Pinocchio

This is the amazing story of a puppet and his creator who
have many adventures.

One day, Geppetto, who earned his living making puppets for travelling theatres, started to carve a puppet out of a piece of wood from a tree which had blown down in a gale. It was very easy to carve that special piece of wood and, as he happily worked away, he pictured in his mind the sort of son he would like to have.

Miraculously, the puppet he created
was the exact image of the son he
longed for. Geppetto was amazed.
"He looks just like the son of my dreams,"
he cried. "What lovely, rosy cheeks he has."
Suddenly the puppet seemed to move.
That was not possible! But it was. Before
Geppetto could stop him, the puppet ran into
the street and started jumping over anything
that got in his way. People in the street look
on in astonishment as Geppetto ran after the
puppet calling,
"Come here, Pinocchio. Do as you are told."

He called the puppet Pinocchio, as that had always been his favourite name. When he caught up with the boy, Geppetto hugged him and called him "son". Then, as Pinocchio seemed to be always moving around, Geppetto decided to tighten all his nuts and bolts so that he would not fall apart. This was not very pleasant for the little one and when Geppetto started to tighten the joint in his neck, he called out,

"Be careful, Daddy! You are hurting me."

"It's a miracle!" exclaimed Geppetto. "He speaks just like a real child."

Afterwards, he dressed the boy in smart, red shorts and a blue shirt. He would have to make sure that Pinocchio received a good education so that he would grow up to be successful. The next morning, Geppetto sold his only winter coat so that he could buy all the books and pencils Pinocchio needed to take to school.

"Be a good boy at school," said Geppetto as he kissed the boy goodbye.

On the way to school, Pinocchio met two naughty boys who, on seeing his brand-new books, offered to buy them from him. Pinocchio readily agreed and, with the money, he bought a ticket to see a show at a nearby theatre.

The show began. Several puppets dressed in a variety of costumes came on stage and danced. In his enthusiasm Pinocchio leaped up to join them and started dancing too. The audience loved it and clapped wildly, showering him with coins.

Noting how popular he was, the owner of the theatre gave Pinocchio three gold coins on condition that he performed every day. Geppetto would be very disappointed if he knew what Pinocchio was doing. The boy was not turning out as he had hoped. Worse was to follow because, after leaving the theatre, Pinocchio did not go home. Instead he wandered around, marvelling at all the sights but soon night began to fall.

Suddenly, two scoundrels, a fox who passed himself off
as a cripple and a cat who pretended to be blind,
approached the puppet and started to ask him questions.
Pinocchio boasted that he was a dancer in the theatre
and that he had three gold coins.   He even showed them
the money so they would not think he was making it up.

The two rascals continued talking to Pinocchio and soon they had convinced him not to trust the theatre owner, saying that they knew him well and, that although he had been generous that day in order to gain Pinocchio's confidence, he would soon stop paying him.

"Come with us," said the fox. "You'll not only have a good time but we'll make you rich as well."

"And famous," added the cat. They even invited him to dinner.

Pinocchio willingly followed the two rogues. The dinner was splendid but when it was finished the two villains cunningly escaped through a window and left poor Pinocchio to pay for the banquet with one of his gold coins. He had had the first important lesson of his life but would he learn from it? Remembering his good father, he decided to return home. The night was very dark so he was a little frightened when he saw two figures approaching.

The figures had blankets over their heads with small holes cut at eye level. An owl, who had been snoozing on a branch of a nearby tree, started screeching. The wise owl had guessed what was about to happen and was trying to warn the little puppet. As it feared, the figures robbed him of everything he had.

The hooded figures turned out to be the two rogues who had tricked Pinocchio before. This time they tied him up and left him hanging upside down from the branch of a tree.

Luckily for Pinocchio, the owl took pity on him and, with great difficulty, managed to free him. This was very good of the owl as, normally, owls are shy creatures and keep away from strangers. It then carried Pinocchio to its home in the nearby tree.

The Blue Fairy, who only appeared in times of trouble, was waiting for Pinocchio when he arrived at the owl's home. She began asking him questions but Pinocchio, trying to sound important, answered her with lies. With each lie, his nose grew a little longer until it was enormous. As the Blue Fairy listened to him, she realised that Pinocchio had forgotten all about his father and had not even considered how worried he would be.

She interrupted the puppet.

"I know that you are telling lies," she said angrily. "I can see everything and know everything. At this very moment your good father is risking his life searching for you along the cliffs."

At last, Pinocchio realised the error of his ways and promised that he would be good in future. He even cried a little.

The fairy forgave him and, with a sweep of her wand, she changed his nose back to its proper size. She told him to go at once in search of Geppetto and he promised to do just that. The owl and the other birds showed their delight by chirping merrily. But did Pinocchio really mean what he said?

He did at the time but all his good intentions came to nothing when he was spotted by a street urchin. Pinocchio refused to go along with him but in the end he had no choice.

"Hurry up", said the street urchin. "The stagecoach to
Fun City will be passing soon. You will really enjoy it
there."
When the stagecoach arrived it was full of naughty, lazy
boys and with much pushing Pinocchio and his new friend
managed to climb aboard.

Pinocchio was astonished when he noticed the ears of some of the boys. They were very, very long. Then to his dismay he realised that his own ears were growing and he was beginning to look like a donkey.

Pinocchio decided that it would be a good idea to escape from a city where little boys turned into donkeys so that unscrupulous men could parade them at fairs for people to make fun of. Luckily for him, as he was trying to escape, his friend, the owl, appeared and saved him.

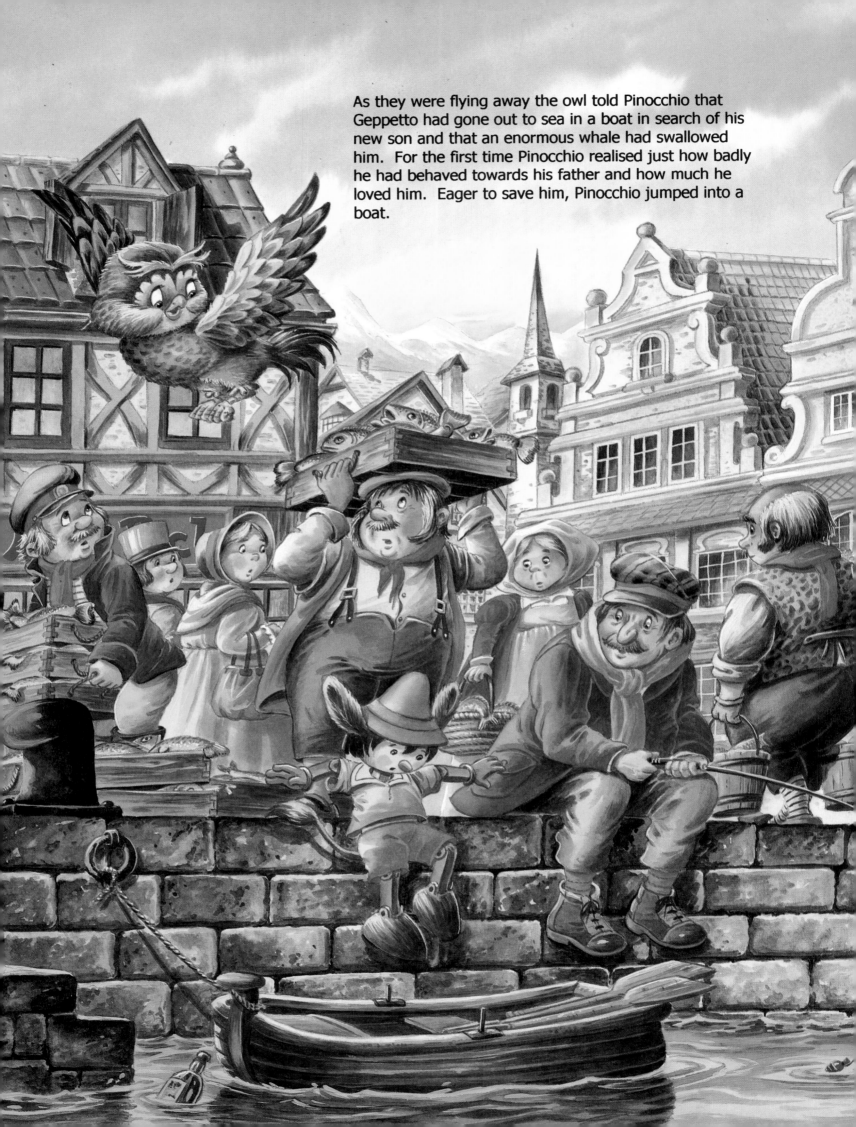

As they were flying away the owl told Pinocchio that Geppetto had gone out to sea in a boat in search of his new son and that an enormous whale had swallowed him. For the first time Pinocchio realised just how badly he had behaved towards his father and how much he loved him. Eager to save him, Pinocchio jumped into a boat.

How difficult it was to make progress as the huge waves threatened to capsize the boat! The sea became more choppy and eventually the fragile boat was engulfed by water. The enormous whale that had swallowed Geppetto was lurking nearby and quickly swallowed Pinocchio as well.

Pinocchio could not believe his eyes for there was Geppetto sitting in his boat. Overjoyed, he threw himself into his father's arms. Realising that Geppetto was very weak, Pinocchio vowed to save him at all costs. Luckily, the light from the boat's lantern enabled him to search for something to help them to escape.

As it swallowed just about everything that got in its way, there were many strange things in the whale's stomach. Pinocchio picked up an oar and tickled the whale's throat with it. This made the monster cough loudly and as it did so Pinocchio grabbed his father and they both shot out of the whale's mouth.

Pinocchio tried to carry Geppetto to the surface but he was too heavy. They were both getting weaker by the minute and Pinocchio was afraid that they were going to drown. Suddenly a dolphin appeared and sent them flying up to the surface and they drifted on to a sandy beach.

Oh, no! His father was not breathing and Pinocchio burst into tears, blaming himself for his death. But help was at hand for, at that moment, the Blue Fairy came flying through the air and, smiling at the little puppet, touched the old man with her magic wand. Geppetto opened his eyes and so the great love he had for his son was rewarded.

After restoring Geppetto to life the Blue Fairy touched the puppet with her magic wand and changed him into a real, live boy. Now the good man really had a proper son, the most loving that ever lived.

Alice in Wonderland

This is the story of a young girl's adventure in Wonderland and of the strange people she meets there.

One beautiful, summer's day, Alice and her older sister, Anna, were spending the afternoon in the country. Anna was reading a book but Alice was beginning to feel bored when suddenly she saw a White Rabbit go racing by. He was a very strange sight, with his top hat and tails and his little briefcase, and he kept repeating over and over again that he was late.

Where could he be going in such a hurry? Alice
jumped up and ran after him and saw him
disappear down a hole in an old tree trunk. The
trunk seemed to be glowing strangely and, without
any hesitation, Alice followed the White Rabbit
down the hole. What folly!

Although the hole did not look very deep, Alice
began to feel dizzy as she realised that, rather
than falling, she was floating gently down,
surrounded by a pale light.

Down she went after the rabbit and at the bottom
she landed in a fireplace. When she finally
managed to climb out she saw the White Rabbit
running away in fright. Who or what could he be
frightened of? Alice could not see anyone and
wondered why the White Rabbit was afraid.

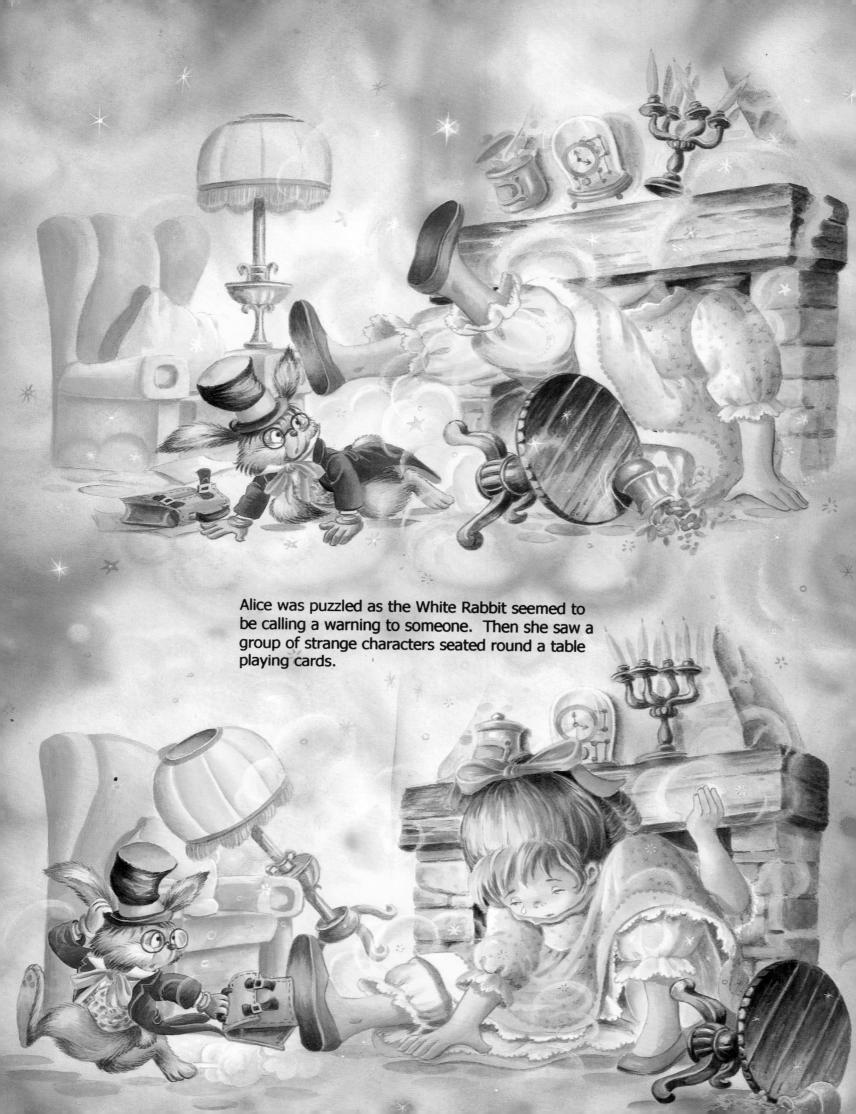

Alice was puzzled as the White Rabbit seemed to be calling a warning to someone. Then she saw a group of strange characters seated round a table playing cards.

"A monster is chasing me," shouted the White Rabbit. A parrot dressed as a pirate shouted an order and the group immediately left their game and re-appeared pulling a heavy cannon.

It was very strange. Alice wondered where this monster could be. Were all these creatures mad? How frightening was the one-armed pirate with his hook! Suddenly, Alice realised that she was the monster they were threatening.

Alice was certain that they were her enemies and
now, for some strange reason, she began to grow
and grow. She looked wildly about her for a place
to hide but neither the undergrowth nor the little
cottage could protect her.

Her enemies had, at last, managed to turn the cannon in her direction and, just when she thought her end had come, a large butterfly appeared and gave her a berry.

"Eat it quickly," it said, and she was so bewildered that she did as she was told.

As soon as she had eaten it something incredible happened. She began to shrink! Now she was more afraid than ever and to make matters worse a loud explosion sounded in the distance. This frightened the strange creatures so much that they forgot about their cannon and approached Alice as they could see that she was very upset.

A little shy at first, they asked her who she was and what she was doing there. Then Alice caught a glimpse of the White Rabbit just behind her trying to run away without being seen. What could he be escaping from?

Without a second thought Alice ran after him
through a strange wood where the trees had faces
and arm-shaped branches on which perched
funny, unusual birds.
"Where on earth am I?" she wondered.

In spite of her weird surroundings, Alice continued to chase the White Rabbit. Just when she thought she could not run any further she came to a clearing in the wood where a very strange group of characters was seated round a table. They were obviously having a party to celebrate something. When they saw Alice, they welcomed her warmly.

After staring at her curiously for a while, they
invited her to join the party. When she asked
what they were celebrating they laughed foolishly
and said,
"What? The elephant's NON-BIRTHDAY, of
course."

Everyone played a musical instrument except the White Rabbit, who was hiding under the table. The elephant, being the host, invited Alice to dance to the sound of the music that his friends were playing. Not knowing how to refuse Alice agreed, albeit somewhat reluctantly.

Alice was pleasantly surprised that the strange creatures were so friendly to her. They offered her plates of doughnuts and cakes, as well as a cup of delicious, hot chocolate and something that tasted of strawberries and apples.

Because everyone was concentrating on the feast the White Rabbit decided that it was a good time to make his escape and ran off thinking that no one would notice his absence. But Alice did notice and she immediately jumped up and ran after him leaving the others open-mouthed with astonishment.

After a while, Alice realised that she had lost the
White Rabbit. Luckily, another strange character,
a caterpillar in fancy dress, showed her a door
which led out of the mysterious forest.

On opening the door, Alice looked carefully around her before venturing over the threshold. To her surprise, there were two soldiers on guard wearing playing cards over their uniforms. They did not speak to Alice but one of them took her by the arm.

They led Alice through another door into a beautiful garden belonging to the King and Queen of this strange land. The White Rabbit was also there, accusing Alice of some wicked deed.

The King did not speak but the Queen insisted on playing croquet. What an odd game! The mallets were flamingos and the balls were hedgehogs.

Poor Alice! As she attempted to hit the hedgehog with the flamingo, she missed and accidentally hit the Queen in the face. The soldiers looked on in amazement.

Suddenly, the White Rabbit rushed forward and accused Alice of hitting the Queen deliberately. He ordered the soldiers to arrest her, while the Queen fell to the floor, almost crushing one of the soldiers.

Then everyone went to the courtroom and Alice was put on trial. The Queen was the judge and she found poor Alice guilty. Alice protested that she had had no-one to defend her but that only made matters worse and the Queen sentenced her to be thrown in to the dungeons.

The soldiers were very cruel to Alice as they took her away, so she decided to escape from them. If she did not do it now she would not be able to escape once she was locked in the dungeons.

On turning a corner she suddenly started running as fast as her legs would carry her. The soldiers chased after her, but soon she began to realise that she was leaving them behind and she was aware of a light glowing around her.

She awoke with a start. Her head was spinning
but she soon realised that all the strange
characters she had met had disappeared.
 "Oh, thank goodness! It was all a bad dream,"
she said. "I think I will be like Anna and read my
book."

Peter Pan

This is a fantastic story of things both real and imagined, good and bad,
where eventually good triumphs.

It was a calm night over the city. High in the sky the stars shone and twinkled. In the Darling household, the three children, John, Michael and Wendy, were reading a book about their favourite hero, Peter Pan.

Suddenly, a silver star shot across the sky and Wendy, followed by her brothers and Nana, the dog, ran to the window.

"That shooting star must have come from Never Never Land where Peter Pan lives," said Wendy.

Mrs. Darling, who had just entered the room, told them firmly that Peter Pan did not exist.

But Mrs. Darling was wrong because at that moment Peter Pan was perched on the roof above the window. He remained silent, listening carefully, until he was sure that Mrs. Darling, after having tucked the children into bed, had left the room.

Quietly, he jumped into the room through the open window, accompanied as always by Tinkerbell, his faithful friend. However, Wendy thought that she heard a noise and got out of bed.

She woke her brothers.
"I'm sure there is someone in the room," said John. They looked around and saw Peter Pan rummaging through the chest of drawers. He was looking for the mischievous Tinkerbell who was hiding there.

The Darling children were overjoyed that their visitor was their hero, Peter Pan. They listened, spellbound, to his stories of life in Never Never Land.

"Why don't you come with me to Never Never Land," said Peter. The children agreed at once and Tinkerbell sprinkled them with magic dust so that they could fly.

"How marvellous," shouted the children as they soared high into the sky amidst the chimney-stacks and bell-towers. Led by Peter Pan, they flew hand in hand and soon they were approaching Never Never Land.

They rested on a cloud for a while so that Peter Pan could point out different places to the children. There was the Mermaid's cave, the Indian village and, anchored in the bay, the big ship of Peter Pan's greatest enemy, Captain Hook. The children could see all kinds of birds flying around, some of them very fierce.

Captain Hook was a pirate and he had hated Peter Pan ever since, in a fierce battle, Peter Pan had cut off Captain Hook's hand and thrown it to a crocodile. Oh, no! The evil pirate looked up and saw Peter.

He ordered his crew to fire the cannon. Peter managed
to avoid the cannonball and told Tinkerbell to take the
children back home where they would be safe.

Tinkerbell argued that it would be better to take them to Peter's home where his animal friends would protect them. Cannonballs continued to fly in all directions but, luckily, Tinkerbell and the children managed to land safely.

Just as they thought they were safe the Indian Chief and his warriors attacked them and took them prisoner. Tinkerbell managed to escape by flying away but what would to happen to the Darling children?

Tinkerbell found Peter Pan and told him what had happened to his friends. Immediately Peter hurried to the Indian camp and the Chief accused Peter of kidnapping his daughter, Heavenly Light.

This was not true and Peter suspected that it was really Captain Hook who had kidnapped the girl, hoping that the Indian Chief would believe that Peter was guilty so that the Indian would join forces with the pirate to overcome Peter Pan.

Captain Hook had taken Heavenly Light to the bottom of the cliff and had tied her to a rock in the sea. She would surely drown when the tide came in. Peter saw her from the top of the cliff and shouted to the Indian Chief to tell him what was happening.

Suddenly, Peter Pan leaped towards Heavenly Light, caught her in his arms and, with the help of his good friends the dolphins and seagulls, threw cruel Captain Hook and his friend into the sea. On seeing this the Indian Chief ran to thank Peter, assuring him that he would never forget what he had done for his daughter. Meanwhile, the mermaids danced merrily in the water.

Heavenly Light's mother was overjoyed to see her daughter but the poor Darling children were still prisoners and were now really frightened. Luckily, as soon as the Indian Chief realised what a mistake he had made he set them free. They all breathed a sigh of relief. They did not want any more adventures like that.

Peter Pan smoked the pipe of peace with the Indian Chief and the children left the camp accompanied by several friendly animals. Wendy assured her brothers that they were safe now.

But she was wrong. Captain Hook never gave up and he had ordered his pirates to set a trap for the children and they captured them in a net and tied them up.

The pirates took the children back to their ship and put a blindfold on poor Wendy. The pirates laughed and told the children that they were all going to drown.

To make matters worse, they were forcing Wendy to walk the plank. Just as one of the pirates was about to push her off, Peter miraculously appeared, swinging from a rope, and knocked the pirate down.

Peter Pan had come to the rescue just in time. He pushed Captain Hook overboard and the Indian Chief helped to dispose of the other pirates in the same way.

Peter allowed the defeated pirates to row to a deserted island where they would have to live on their own and would not be able to harm anyone else.

As the pirates disappeared in the distance Peter Pan decided that it was time the Darling children returned home. Tinkerbell sprinkled her magic dust all over the pirate ship and it soared into the air. In no time at all they arrived back home.

After saying goodbye to the children, Peter Pan and Tinkerbell flew back to Never Never Land.
"We must have dreamt the whole thing," said John.
"Impossible," said Wendy. "Just look at the feathers that we are wearing on our heads."

Snow White

This is the story of a beautiful Princess who is persecuted
by her wicked stepmother and of her seven faithful little
friends.

Once upon a time there lived a Princess called Snow White whose mother had died. Her father, the King, re-married and, although he thought she was kind and good, his new wife was really very evil. When he too died, Snow White was at the mercy of her wicked stepmother.

The Queen was a wicked witch and treated Snow White
cruelly. She was very vain and every morning would look
in her magic mirror and say,
"Who is the fairest in the land?"
The mirror would always reply,
"You are the fairest."

One fateful morning the mirror answered,
"Snow White is the fairest in all the land."
At these words the Queen flew into a terrible rage and,
calling her huntsman to her, ordered him to take Snow
White into the forest and kill her.

The huntsman took
Snow White into the forest
but he could not kill her.
He told her to run away as far
as she could so that the Queen would
never find out that she was still alive.

Snow White was very grateful to the huntsman for giving her the chance to escape and, after thanking him, she began to run. On and on she ran through the forest until, as night fell, she lay down and slept.

The friendly creatures of the forest watched over the young girl for they had never seen anyone like her before. Early next morning, awakened by the chirping of the birds, Snow White suddenly noticed a tiny cottage not far away. She went to the door and knocked. There was no answer so she went inside.

The forest creatures went with her into the cottage.
"Is anyone there?" she called but no-one answered and
she saw, lying neatly on a table, seven little bowls, food
and water and was so hungry that she ate the food and
hoped the owners of the cottage would not mind. Now
she felt really tired. If only she could rest! Sleeping on
the hard ground had not been very comfortable!

Guided by the fawn she climbed the stairs. At the top was a bedroom with seven little beds. She lay down across three of them and, watched over by the friendly fawn, she fell asleep.

She slept for several hours, in fact until night fell once more. Meanwhile, seven little men were marching home towards the cottage after a hard day's work in a diamond mine.

When they arrived at the cottage door they found that it was open.

"There must be someone inside," they cried. "Come on, let's find the intruder."

Once inside they saw that their dinner had been eaten.
One behind the other they stealthily climbed the stairs.
"Look at this," said one of the little men, on discovering
Snow White asleep across three of the beds.

Suddenly Snow White woke up. She was very frightened when she saw the seven dwarves around her but they looked at her with such kindness that her fear vanished instantly. The dwarves thought she was very beautiful and, when the oldest of the seven asked her who she was, she told them her story.

The dwarves took pity on her. They decided to let her live in their cottage with them and, in return, she would clean the cottage and cook their meals while they were out working in the mine.

Snow White quickly settled in her new home and the
dwarves were very happy to have her with them. They
danced and sang and even the forest animals joined in.

But their happiness would not last because, far away, the cruel Queen consulted her magic mirror and discovered that Snow White was still alive. She flew into a rage and decided that she herself must kill Snow White.

She cast a magic spell to disguise herself as a gypsy and then mixed a poisonous potion which she injected into a rosy, red apple.

The Queen made her way through the forest to Snow White's new home. She hid behind a tree and waited. Eventually, the dwarves came out of the cottage and marched off to work. Now it was time to put her plan into action.

When the gypsy knocked on the door, Snow White did not realise that it was her stepmother in disguise. She accepted the juicy, red apple which the gypsy offered but after taking one bite fell to the ground.

The evil Queen laughed in glee but suddenly all the animals of the forest flung themselves at her. They pushed her into a deep ravine from which she was unable to escape and she starved to death.

Then the animals ran as quickly as they could to the diamond mine to tell the seven dwarves what had happened. They immediately threw down their tools and hurried to the aid of their little friend. Would they be in time?

The dwarves rode swiftly to the cottage on the backs of the kind forest creatures but as soon as they saw Snow White lying motionless they knew that they were too late to help her. She was dead and they were beside themselves with grief.

They decided she should have a proper tomb and they worked together to make her a satin-lined, glass coffin so they would always be able to look at her. They pretended that she was only sleeping and that one day she would wake up.

When it was finished they carried the coffin to a beautiful forest glade where sunshine filtered through the branches of the trees and the ground was covered with brightly-coloured flowers. But nothing could ease their grief and pain.

Time passed and one day a handsome Prince rode by on a white charger. When he saw the coffin surrounded by the seven dwarves he was intrigued. When the dwarves told him the sad story he immediately fell in love with the Princess.

The Prince lifted the lid of the glass coffin and gently kissed the Princess and as he did so she sat up and smiled. The dwarves were overjoyed! This was the miracle for which they had hoped.

The Prince and Snow White were married and they lived
happily ever after in a beautiful palace where they were
often visited by the seven dwarves.